Murder at the Pirate Museum

A Harper Rogers Cozy Mystery

Sharon E. Buck

Copyright © 2024 by Sharon E. Buck

All rights reserved.

No portion of this book may be reproduced in any form without written permission from the publisher or author, except as permitted by U.S. copyright law.

This book is a work of fiction. Names, characters, businesses, organizations, places, events, and incidents either are the product of the author's imagination or are used fictitiously. Any resemblance to actual persons, living or dead, events, or locales is entirely coincidental.

For more information, or to book an event, contact : sharon@sharonebuck.com
http://www.SharonEBuck.com

To join my VIP Newsletter and to receive a **FREE** book, go to www.SharonEBuck.com/newsletter

Cover design by Steven Novak, NovakIllustration.com

Looking for a dash of fun, a hint of snark, a sprinkle of sass, and a whole lot of silliness with a Florida twist?

SCAN ME!
To receive a FREE Book

Join my free, no obligation, twice a month newsletter, and I promise not to send your email address to the "your car warranty has expired" people.

SharonEBuck.com

Contents

1. Chapter 1 — 1
2. Chapter 2 — 23
3. Chapter 3 — 38
4. Chapter 4 — 60
5. Chapter 5 — 80
6. Chapter 6 — 91
7. Chapter 7 — 98
8. Chapter 8 — 108
9. Chapter 9 — 121
10. Chapter 10 — 135
11. Chapter 11 — 136

12. Chapter 12	171
13. Chapter 13	183
14. Chapter 14	189
FREE BOOK	191
Harper Rogers Series	192
Parker Bell Series	193
More Books	194
Acknowledgements	195
About the author	200

Chapter 1

I screamed. I felt someone push me and saw something being tossed at me. Since I have the athletic skills of a drunk ninja turtle, I didn't catch it. Clattering to the wooden plank floor was a bloody knife. Next to it was a man lying in a puddle of blood.

I had seen the man when I first entered the Pirate Museum. Thinking he was some St. Augustine timeshare salesman dressed as a pirate, I had ignored him.

Upon looking closer at him, my opinion hadn't changed except to notice that he was dressed more as homeless chic with a blousy dirty shirt and baggy pants. He had long red hair and a pitifully scraggly beard for an adult male.

When I screamed, the other tourists turned toward me. I had already knelt down beside the man to see if I could do anything for him. I also made the incredibly stupid mistake of picking up the knife to move it out of the way when I stood up.

That's what the tourists saw - me with a bloody knife in my hand. Two rather large, dairy-fed women from the Midwest somewhere saw me with the bloody weapon of mass destruction and decided I had killed the man on the floor.

If they had only known the thoughts that were swirling around in my brain looking like Mr. Toad's Wild Ride at Disney World, they wouldn't have bothered trying to save the rest of the tourists in the museum.

They rushed toward me trying to keep me from escaping. I'd like to point out I was standing straight up and had made zero, nada, no attempt to escape, and they started slamming me in my back with their oversized purses apparently filled with boat anchors.

I covered my head with my arms and stumbled forward only to trip over the dead guy, fall, and smack my head on the corner of the display case.

Discovering later at the hospital that I had a concussion and needed three stitches, I'm going to blame everything that happened before the hospital as temporary insanity. Yeah, I'm just going to say I don't remember squat.

***

What I think happened, since I probably had short-term amnesia from the concussion, was, apparently, I continued to scream for help. Evidently, that's not the thing to do in a pirate museum where the cannons periodically erupt with a loud boom and white smoke curls out. It's a tourist thing for someone to scream and the store's staff paid absolutely no attention to the shrieking I was doing.

Not having the sense God gave a goose, I ran out into the store area with the bloody knife in my hand. Yes, there were a lot of tourists wandering around. They pretty much dissipated when they saw me.

The middle-aged cashier blanched, and I saw her push a button under the countertop.

I was blathering and pointing at the inside of the museum. Taking a guess I wasn't making much sense, I turned to go back in and see about the man on the floor when I was attacked again by those two women wielding their boat anchor heavy touristy canvas bags. They continued to whale on me until the cops showed up.

Still prattling on and probably making no sense to anyone, I tried to stand up and explain what had happened when I felt the cold steel handcuffs snap around my wrist. This wasn't good. I had never been arrested before, I was scared, and it occurred to me that I was being arrested for murder. I started to cry. I couldn't even think. My head hurt...and my shoulders...every place those heifer-sized women had hit me with their overloaded bags.

I was yanked unceremoniously up from the floor by a dark blue-uniformed police officer. At least, the women had stopped beating me up with their I Love St.Augustine tourist tote bags.

The cashier had gone back in the hole of the ship's décor and had let loose a blood-curdling scream. "George, George, George! What did she do to you?"

More officers flooded the area. My mind was attempting to mimic a whirling dervish with thoughts that were never going to be formed into complete sentences.

Being pushed roughly into the back of a police cruiser, the officer was not listening to me as blood was running down my face from where I had hit my head on the table corner. My only thought was I didn't want to wear prison orange, that's just not my color.

He did take me to the hospital where I received three stitches and was diagnosed with a concussion.

Finally managing to get my wits to fly in a somewhat uniform manner, I asked, "When do I get my phone call?"

No response. Maybe I didn't speak loud enough. "Hey! When do I get my phone call?"

No one was paying any attention to me. I probably looked like every other crazy person the cops brought to the hospital.

My head hurt. As addled as my brain was, I realized I needed to call for help, and the only phone number I could remember was my best friend Ronnie's. This is what happens when you rely on your cell phone for everything. I'm convinced that part of your memory cells die every time you don't have to recall a phone number.

Now convinced I had no more brain cells left, I was going to end up in prison orange and becoming someone's jailhouse wife.

I threw up. Medical staff assured me it was because that's one of the symptoms of a concussion. I didn't tell them it was from the stress of thinking I was going to be some female prisoner's new special friend...and that I would have to wear orange jumpsuits. I was scared out of my wits...at least the ones that were still intact from not memorizing phone numbers.

At some point, the police did let me call Ronnie.

"Hi, honey, what's happening?" He was chipper.

I started to cry. "Ronnie, I've been arrested over in St. Augustine. Find me an attorney quick."

"Do not, repeat do not, do anything other than give them your name. That's it, nothing else. I'll find you someone who'll get you out. Only your name."

Looking ever the fashionista that I am not, I was back in the police car and hauled off to jail. They put me in a room and not a jail cell.

An officer with a bulbous nose, short salt-and-pepper hair, and having theI've-eaten-way-too-many-doughnuts belly came waddling in the room and plopped down in a chair across the table from me.

"What's your name?"

"HarperRogers."

He sighed, "What's your full name?"

"Harper Elizabeth Rogers."

"Tell me your version of what happened."

"No."This was not a word I used frequently, and it sounded a little unnatural, but I wasn't going to give these yahoos any ammunition to use against me.

"If you don't have anything to hide, why not just tell me what happened?" He sounded bored.

I just looked at him. I'm a writer and I stare for long periods of time at the computer screen, I could keep this up for hours. I was trying to organize my thoughts into a somewhat semblance of order while ignoring him. My head hurt.

If I focused on the new murder mystery book in my brain I was writing, I really could sit and look at this guy for hours, days even. The computer only talks back when I mash a couple of keys. I didn't feel the need to talk. I could feel my body starting to relax a little.

Although I wanted to lie down and go to sleep, I decided to contemplate my day so far.

***

I remembered I was asking myself tons of questions. Did Sir Francis Drake bury his pirate treasure in St. Augustine? Why were there so many pirates in this area? What was their average age? Did they die rich or as a pauper? Did they share the treasure that supposedly every pirate ship had? Who were the female pirates?

All of these and a thousand other questions popped up in my mind as I wandered through the Pirate Museum in St. Augustine. As the oldest city in the United States, it had seen more than its fair share of pirates...Blackbeard, Andrew Ranson, Captain Kid, Sir Francis Drake, and many, many more always looking to plunder whatever valuables they could find.

I remember I had been fascinated with the museum's décor. It held a large collection of artifacts from the seventeen and eighteen hundreds. The museum was designed to look like you were inside a Spanish galleon, dark wood floors with rigging ropes, historical guns, and pottery were carefully secured behind safety where some less-than-honest tourist couldn't put their little grubby fingers on them and heist them back to whatever state they came from.

With over six million people visiting this quaint and oldest city in the United States, smart businesspeople designed their attractions for the tourists to look at things but not be able to touch them.

I was doing research for my new book, and I went to the only museum in the United States that had the largest and most authentic collection of pirate artifacts under roof. Fortunately, it was only about a thirty-five-minute drive from Palm Park.

I had always liked St. Augustine and learning about pirates and their so-called evil ways. It also gave me a great excuse to visit the bakery shop Crème de la Cocoa and get the best macarons ever.

While I was trying to decide if I was hungry or not and needed a macaron fix, I noticed there were signs everywhere alerting tourists that they were being recorded.

My favorite placard warning tourists not to steal anything was:

"Roses are red, violets are blue,

A pirate's heart beats for treasure so true.

With a patch on one eye, and a parrot or two,

I'll chop off a finger or two

If anything disappears with you."

I was chuckling to myself and still debating when I was going to leave for the sugary goodness of a macaron this side of heaven when a long, red-haired, gaunt man with a few wispy red fringes of what was supposed to be a beard sidled up to me. I jumped. I hadn't noticed him. So much for my observational skills.

After living in Jacksonville for a number of years and basically being somewhat paranoid in general, I was convinced that was a good thing for a mystery writer because it added credibility to my books, I glanced at his clothes, they appeared to be homeless chic, and snapped, "Dude, you need to back off."

My mind swirled with different scenarios of what I would do if he tried to attack me. Maybe if I pretended to faint that would work or maybe if I bit him on the nose, he would leave me alone. I saw that in a movie once, or....

"Ah, me lass, you be having a fine time wouldn't you now?"

Oh, mercy, was this a re-enactment or one of the crazies who had escaped cold weather up north and had decided to relocate to sunny, hotter than a fried-egg-on-the-sidewalk, Florida?

I truly don't like engaging in small talk even with friends much less with a total, whacko-looking stranger. I tried ignoring him but, he was persistent. Maybe he was trying to sell me a timeshare while dressed as a pirate. Except, he really didn't look like a pirate. There was absolutely no attempt to dress like a pirate. He had on a way too large blousy shirt that could have been an extra-large from a well-known large discount store with the blue, white, and yellow signage.

His pants looked like they came from Goodwill, and they were baggy. He was also barefoot. He also smelled, I tried not to inhale too deeply but the distinct aroma of garlic and alcohol permeated my olfactory senses. I didn't think he'd had a shower in several days simply because my eyes were starting to water.

How did this crazy person get in here? Maybe an employee let him in and was splitting timeshare commissions or maybe…

See, this is what happens when I've had too much coffee in the morning. It's bad enough that I always have way too many story ideas running loose in my head at any given time but it's even worse when you combine the two together along with my basic up-and-down yo-yo personality.

"Awe, come on, lassie, ye wouldn't be…"

Okay, I'd had enough of this fake dialogue and my fuse, never long to begin with, let loose. "What part of leave me alone do you not understand? I'm a writer, a mystery writer, and I'm trying to do some research on pirates. You're bothering me. Be gone!" I attempted to shoo him away by waving my hands in a dismissive way.

"Ah, me lass, I can be telling you tales that will make your hair and toenails curl."

I shuddered. The very idea of my toenails curling sent my mind reeling back to that iconic scene from "The Wizard of Oz," where the Wicked Witch's toes curled up and vanished beneath the house.

"Where's the director?" I demanded. "I'm reporting you for annoying the customers."

A smile stretched across his face showing fake blackened teeth. I had the horrible thought he might be the director. I was wrong. It was worse.

"Ah, me lass, I'm actually the owner of this wonderful museum celebrating St. Augustinepirates. What would you like to know about pirates?"

I was aghast and before I could stop the words, they escaped from my mouth. "You're kidding, right? You stink. I mean, you literally stink! When was the last time you showered?"

Most normal people would have been appalled but apparently this guy had the social skills of a goat. He laughed.

I could feel my fuse igniting even more. Snarling, "Get out of my way! I'm leaving!"

"Hey, excuse me." Someone was standing behind him and he turned. I whirled around, heading toward the door, hoping the distraction would cause him to leave me alone. I heard a soft oof. Someone jostled me and I semi-turned to see why.

"Here, catch!"

I was so startled at seeing something being tossed at me that I never looked to see where it came from.

Catching anything was not an athletic skill I possessed. That's when I heard the soft oof, looked down, and saw the red-haired guy on the floor.

"Help! Help!" I screamed. There were several other tourists in the museum, who looked over at me, saw the knife, and then they were stampeding for the door shouting and carrying on.

Chapter 2

The police officer must have said something again while I was going over all of the details in my mind. My head hurt and I gingerly touched the bandage over my eye.

"Huh? What did you say?" I asked, glancing around the gray austere room before settling back and looking at the officer.

"I said why aren't you talking?"

"Am I bleeding?" I wasn't sure if the stitches leaked or not.

He didn't say anything.

Blowing air out my nose, "Told you, I don't have to. I'm waiting on my attorney."

Dive bombing back into my brain, whatever information I needed on pirates I could find online. I had only gone to the museum so I could get a feel of what their lives might have been like with the old clothes, guns, and maps.

After looking at those clothes, the texture and the weight of them in the steamy, unairconditioned, humidity of the Sunshine State, I was pretty sure pirates would not have had the most pleasant of personalities. St. Augustine was originally located in the middle of nowhere on the edge of swamps filled with mosquitos, rattlesnakes, and alligators. It would have been a smorgasbord for mosquitoes wanting to feast on a naked arm.

I was trying to figure out the basic plot line of my new book when a woman popped through the door, never looking at the bored officer. "You can go now. I need to talk to my client."

Hurray, Ronnie had come through for me! That's what BFFs are for. She looked vaguely familiar, but I couldn't place her.

Her warm smile put me immediately at ease. "Hi, Harper. Ronnie told me you needed my help."

Nodding borderline frantically, I tried to smile. It probably came out as a grimace.

"You may or may not remember me from high school. I'm A.B. Read."

Frowning slightly, my brain was spinning feverishly trying to put a name and a face together. I wasn't having a whole lot of luck with this. I'm blaming it on the stress factor of sitting in jail and being blamed for a crime I didn't commit.

"I went by Anne in those days." Her smile was bigger. She had placed her briefcase on the table and pulled out a legal pad. "Give me the short version of what happened."

Not caring what her name was umpteen years ago, I was only concerned about me, myself, and I getting out of here.

I told her everything, she nodded, standing up, "Give me a moment."

Oh, great! Now I've been left alone in this room with nothing to focus my thoughts on except...nothingness. I laid my head on my arms on the table. I went to sleep. Stress will do that to me. Also, a concussion will do that as well.

It was probably another hour before Mr. Personality opened the door and motioned for me to follow him.

A.B. was standing at the police countertop, smiled, and said, "Come on."

I must have looked confused.

"It's time to go home." She turned and I followed her to the parking lot.

"Um, A.B., do you think you could give me a ride home?"

She laughed, a little twinkling-type of laugh. "You don't think I'm going to leave you out here in the parking lot, do you?"

Neither one of us talked in the car. I almost ran to my apartment. I couldn't wait to get in the shower and wash the nastiness of the past twenty-four hours off. I gave serious thought to throwing away the clothes I had been wearing, but I'm parsimonious and didn't want to get rid of perfectly good clothes.

What does parsimonious mean? I'm cheaper than dirt, also known as what is the real value of something that I'm willing to part money for from my tightly clenched little fist.

Hearing a knock at the door. I peeked through the keyhole. I was surprised to see Detective Sam Needles standing there. Sam and I had dined together on several occasions. I wouldn't call it dating exactly, it was more along the lines of friends with no benefits.

Did I mention he was cute? Dark hair, dimples, and a killer smile.

"Hey, Sam," I smiled as I opened the door, "what's up?"

He wasn't smiling. "Were you at the Pirate Museum in St. Augustine earlier today?"

So much for a warm and fuzzy hello.

"Yes." I was puzzled.

Sam cleared his throat. "Harper, did you have an argument with George Cloise?"

"Who?"

"The pirate museum owner." Sam wasn't smiling. A faint tingling of less-than-positive vibes was making its way through my body. I wondered if I should be calling my attorney.

"That's his name?" I was stalling for time. "I didn't have an argument with him. He was being annoying. Do I need to call my attorney?"

He frowned, "What is the bandage on your head for?"

"I fell and hit my head on a display table. There are three beautiful stitches under the bandage. Why are you asking me these questions? Anything that happened yesterday was in St. Augustine, not Palm Park."

"I know. I heard it through the grapevine and…"

Laughing, I said, "Marvin Gaye. I know that song."

Shaking his head and closing his eyes, his mouth turned into a grin. "That was a bad choice of words. Hopefully, this doesn't mean I need to dance now."

"No." We were both laughing and headed to sit on the couch. "So, what are you really doing here?"

He shifted his weight on the couch and crossed one leg over the other. He appeared to be a little nervous.

"Just thought I'd come over and see how you were."

My brows furrowed and my eyes narrowed. I was suspicious. Had Sam been sent over to see what information he could obtain from me about that debacle in St. Augustine?

Clearing his throat, he said, "I heard you were the last one in the museum?"

"Oh, not true! Not true!" I borderline shrieked. I almost jumped up from the sofa. "There were two tourists in there who started beating me up with their purses. There's no way I was the last person in there!"

I was breathing deeply, and I was mad.

"Your fingerprints were found on the knife, and…" Sam paused, "you were seen on tape shoving him."

I stood there, blinking. He was a spy. He had been sent to see what other information he could get.

"Are you arresting me?" I was trying to sound brave when every fiber of my being was screaming "I can't go to jail. I don't look good in orange."

Sam shook his head. "No, of course not. You are a person of interest in this case." He stood up. "Don't think about leaving Palm Park."

I could only nod. I felt immobilized. Sam left. I was still standing in the middle of my living room and knew I needed a salted caramel macaron I had stashed in my freezer. There was a black vortex swirling around in my brain sucking out any coherent thoughts.

Why was George murdered? I crunched down on my brain cells while savoring the macaron to see if I remembered who was standing behind him. Much as I hate to admit it, I was probably too self-absorbed to even notice what other tourists were looking at the pirate artifacts. It's bad enough I can be that obtuse in general but it's even worse when I'm researching something, which is what I was doing.

The delicious sugar concoction I was holding in my hand found its way to my mouth. I could feel the velvety softness almost melting in my mouth. Maybe it was the sugar burst winding its way through my body or maybe my brain cells had kicked back into gear.

I called A.B. Searching through long-ago memories, she and I had gone to high school together, I vaguely remembered she'd scored a perfect SAT score for the whole state of Florida, causing a great deal of stress amongst the educated elite in the school system because they were sure it couldn't be done. She proved them wrong. What was even funnier was she was from Palm Park, a rural, economically depressed little town on the beautiful St. Johns River in northeast Florida. No one expected anything like this from Palm Park.

She had won numerous scholarships and graduated magna cum laude from the prestigious University of Florida Law School. Why she had come back to Palm Park was beyond me, she could have practiced anywhere and probably made a lot more money.

"A.B. Read Law Office." The voice was crisp, sharp, and had that gatekeeper attitude.

I didn't like attorneys in general. They always seemed to be so smug that they were smarter than you. Bad memories of my Jacksonville divorce attorney surfaced; although I had to be fair, she did keep my ex-husband from benefiting from my intellectual property. I probably would have killed everyone in sight had I had to share my book royalties with him.

"Um, this is Harper Rogers. May I speak with Anne? We went to high school together."

"She goes by A.B. now. Let me check to see if she's available." Attorney speak for "Let me see if she wants to talk to you."

I didn't have to wait long. "Hey, Harper, how are you doing?"

I relaxed and started to tell her about Sam showing up and asking questions when she interrupted me. "Come in at nine tomorrow morning and we'll talk.

Oh, bring four glazed doughnuts with you. Brenda will love you for it."

Indulging in watching "Funny Girl" with Barbra Streisand for the two thousand and twenty-ninth time, I had a very peaceful evening at home.

Chapter 3

Entering through the heavy doors, I vaguely wondered why so many law offices have hard-to-open doors. Maybe they're just making sure you really want to hire them.

The lobby area was very tastefully appointed, a fancy word for decorated, with expensively framed artwork depicting various scenes from the St. Johns River, St. Augustine's Castillo de San Marcos, and, what's this? A painting of female pirates Anne Bonny and Mary Read? That's interesting.

Anne or A.B. entered the lobby, smiling and holding out her hands. "Harper, so nice to see you again. This time not at the jail."

Grinning slightly, I handed her the four glazed doughnuts. Her smile became even bigger, and her blue eyes sparkled. "Why, thank you so very much, Harper. Brenda, two for you, and bring the other two into the office."

A.B. turned and I followed her. I stopped once I walked through the door. Her office had numerous paintings of Anne Bonny, Mary Read, Grace O'Malley, and a few other female pirates I didn't know hung on the walls. There appeared to be a number of pirate-type artifacts in glass display cases around the room. To say she was enamored with female pirates was an understatement. I was impressed.

In fact, the office was decorated to look like a captain's cabin. This was every bit as nice if not better than the Pirate Museum's décor.

A.B. took a seat at the round ruff hewn wood table next to a massive ornately carved wood desk. I sat down to her left.

Behind the desk was a pirate ship that appeared to be bobbing up and down on the St. Johns River. I don't know how that was done but it certainly gave the appearance that pirates may be close by.

Of course, maybe it was a warning to clients that they had better make sure they paid their invoices on time or maybe it was simply a reminder that women could be every bit as intimidating and in control of their destiny as male pirates.

Smiling, she said, "Welcome to my world. Now, tell me everything."

I proceeded with everything that had happened and ended with Sam ordering me not to leave Palm Park.

"They don't have enough evidence to arrest you or they would have. They're merely trying to put the fear of God into you. If they have the tape of you shoving George, someone tossing something to you, then the tape will show everything."

"Here's the thing, A.B., only one person was watching the cash register at the entrance. There were a lot of tourists in the shop and the museum."

We chatted a few more minutes catching up on our lives since high school, I wrote her a modest retainer check in case anything happened and left feeling a little better.

Stopping by my friend Ronnie's pet store, I knew I could always hug one of the little Maltese puppies he had in the shop. They were such a little bundle of joy and love all wrapped up in baby soft hair. If it weren't for the fact that I'd be an awful puppy mama, I'd have a dozen of them.

Ronnie swears I would forget to feed them and take them out to do their business. Unfortunately, he's right. When I'm in the midst of writing a new book, I'm pretty much oblivious to anything else.

I have to order take-out most of the time simply because I've burned so much food on the stovetop and in the oven that even my cleaning lady doesn't want to clean it. Martha Stewart doesn't have to worry about my domestic skills upsetting her as the queen of all things domestic.

Although my ex-husband never mentioned my lack of housekeeping aptitude in the divorce, it was the standard "irreconcilable differences", I'd like to point out the man simply expected dishes of food to be placed on the coffee table and then they disappeared when he was through eating. He had no clue on how to do anything in the kitchen…or the garage…or the yard…or…you get the idea. He did, on the other hand, know how to find a sweet young thing who thought he was the greatest thing since sliced bread. I was more than willing to let her have him at this point. I don't know what we ever saw in each other, but we parted amicably.

"Oh, honey, honey!" Ronnie rushed toward me with his arms outstretched for a hug. He was almost as much fun as the little furbabies he had in his store. Bussing me on both cheeks, he leaned back and said, "What's going on? I can feel it. Harper Elizabeth Rogers, no keeping secrets from me…because you can't!" We both laughed.

Here's a little background on me before we go any further. My mother had a wicked sense of humor because, yes, my initials do spell HER. That is certainly preferable to dear old dad wanting to name me Harper Olivia Rogers aka HOR. As my mother explained many years later, she wasn't going to have a daughter where the initials spelled out an euphonism for a common street walker.

Ronnie was chattering up a storm, picking up and handing me little white wiggly puppies who couldn't kiss me enough. I was in love and every time I came to the shop, I swooned over them again and again.

Finally, holding one of the precious little ones next to my heart, I told Ronnie what had happened at the pirate museum.

I think Ronnie knew virtually any important person in what I fondly referred to as the Northeast Florida version of the Bermuda Triangle – Jacksonville, Palm

Park, and St. Augustine. It seems like I was always going out from Palm Park to either Jacksonville or St. Augustine and then being snapped back to Palm Park like a rubber band that had been stretched too tight.

"Honey, you've got to tell me what happened! George was looney tunes to begin with and had absolutely no fashion sense." He sniffed.

I laughed silently. This was coming from a man who was wearing black and silver striped pants with a black vest and white shirt with a little red western string tie, and black ankle boots.

"I take it you didn't like him," I grinned.

"Oh, he was okay. He just wouldn't dress like a pirate and, honestly, if it weren't for Vykky deBurgo, the museum wouldn't exist."

My ears picked up and my internal radar started spinning around like sugar in a cotton candy machine. There was a story here, I just knew it.

"Tell me more, tell me more," I singsonged at him, smiling.

"Oh, honey, you're such a wonderful person but please don't sing. You can't carry a tune in a bucket." Ronnie rolled his eyes and giggled.

I couldn't argue with him on that. It was true. I could sing four notes on key, but they weren't necessarily all together at the same time.

"Are you going to tell me the low down or are you going to make me pull those silly

Christmas lights out of that thing you call a beard?" I laughed.

He pretended to be hurt but I knew better. Ronnie had found some sparkly battery-operated lights online that he could put in his beard. Always the fashionista.

"Vykky deBurgo is a member of one of the founding families of St. Augustine and…"

"Let me guess, she spells her name in a unique way." I rolled my eyes. In my limited experience, I had discovered folks of a certain upper echelon evidently wanted to be thought of as very special and, thus, spelled their names in an uncommon fashion.

Wiggling his bushy black eyebrows, "But, of course, my darlin'. Her real name is Victoria, and she goes by V-y-k-k-y."

Scooping up one of the bouncy Maltese puppies and touching his nose to her nose, "Vykky is the patron saint of the museum. George used to be a diver and went on numerous treasure-hunting dives with a lot of famous people including Mel Fisher.

"George had the artifacts but no money to set up the museum and he was truly convinced the public, and especially the tourists, would be willing to pay money to see his pirate treasures."

"Well, he was right, I suppose." Although the people in the store and the museum I saw didn't equate to him being a rich man with this particular business venture but, then again, I could be wrong, and it could have been just to be a slow day when I was there.

"Think about it, Harper, there are more than six million visitors to St. Augustine every year, and even if only one percent of them go to the museum, George's making somewhere in the one million two hundred thousand range. That's not too shabby and a great return on investment."

"This doesn't make any sense, Ronnie. If he's making that type of money, what does he need Vykky for?"

Smiling, "Remember, she set him up in business. She's probably getting half of whatever he's making. So…"

"So, she's a smart businesswoman," I finished for him.

Ronnie was so dramatic. Looking to his left, then to his right, leaned forward, and whispered, "She's looking for a specific type of treasure."

I laughed. "Ronnie, you know the puppies aren't going to tell anyone, right?"

He looked a little sheepish.

"What kind of treasure is she looking for? I would think she would have found it by now."

He shrugged.

The bell over the door tinkled letting us know that someone had entered the store.

It was Sam. Usually he was smiling when he saw us. This was not one of those times.

"Harper Rogers, you're under arrest for the murder of George Cloise."

I ceased to breathe, there was no oxygen in the air, and I was pretty sure my eyes had rolled back in my head giving the appearance of a dead person. Ronnie told me later no such thing had occurred and that I had laughed when Sam told me that.

Isn't it funny how the same incident can cause two different perceptions from two people witnessing the exact same thing and both of them be right? I'm guessing that these different perceptions of life are what cause eyewitness descriptions to be notoriously unreliable in the law enforcement field.

Trying to be funny, I stuck both arms out and grinned. "Okay, go ahead and slap my wrists now."

Sam obviously doesn't have the same sense of humor I have because the man actually slapped handcuffs on me before I could retract my outstretched arms.

As he proceeded to read me my Miranda rights, as shocked as I was, I did manage to eke out, "Ronnie, call A.B., tell her I've been arrested again, and that I don't look good in orange." This last part I almost wailed.

"She doesn't, you know," said Ronnie, turning to Sam.

Sam blinked his eyes a couple of times. "She doesn't what?"

"Really, Sam, you don't know this?" Ronnie sounded almost exasperated. "Harper doesn't look good in orange."

Shaking his head in disbelief, he probably couldn't fathom how both Ronnie and I agreed that I did not look good in orange because it clashed terribly with my pale complexion. If I were being realistic, he probably thought we were both looney tunes looking for our own reality TV show.

My emotions were swirling like crazy: disbelief, shock, anger, and total confusion. How could this possibly be? I'm the good girl who never gets into trouble. Just because I've had a couple of murders happen near me since I moved back to Palm Park doesn't count. I've lived for years with nothing nefarious happening anywhere close to me. Palm Park must be a weird vortex of some off-the-chart quantum physics and they, for some reason, have attached themselves to my energy vibrations. Yeah, that sounds a little woo-woo. Even I don't think I buy into that explanation.

My only real explanation is maybe I've been good for way too long and strange things just happen in life. Although, admittedly, I don't think most people have these types of occurrences in their lifetime. Maybe it's come about because I'm a mystery writer and I need new things to write about.

Do I dare admit that these thoughts are zooming through my brain at the speed of Superman jumping over a locomotive?

"Harper, how many times do I have to tell you to get a move on?" Sam sounded irritated although he wasn't making a move to drag me kicking and screaming out to the squad car. I'm not prone to screaming and kicking in general. It's not a becoming look for a child, and certainly not for an adult.

"I don't want it to look like you're resisting arrest. That won't look good in the report."

He had me there. If this ever went to court, it definitely wouldn't endear me to the judge.

"Ronnie, call A.B." I was urging him to hurry up. I didn't want to spend the night again in jail which, unfortunately, is what happened before A.B. could get me bailed out. It takes hours to get sprung once you're thrown in jail.

The good news was there were several prostitutes in the holding cell. While some folks refer to them as ladies of the evening, I will testify that these women were not ladies in any sense of the word. They were foul-mouthed, stunk, and were dressed every bit as bad as what you might suspect. These women were not highly paid escorts, they were low-level street walkers where the cops used them to make their monthly quota of arrests.

Once they discovered I was a writer, yes, I told them hoping no one would beat me up, they told me some great stories – many of them funny. They all asked if I would put them in one of my books. Of course! They could become new readers and buy my books. Also, my premise was they wouldn't hurt me if I promised to put them in a book.

A.B. escorted me out of jail again six hours later and took me home. She didn't say much, I didn't say much. All I really wanted to do was take a long hot shower. I wondered if all the negativity of these two jail experiences could be washed off my body, find its way down the drain, and out of my life.

Crawling into bed although it was now daylight, something tickled my brain that Ronnie had said. Vykky was the patron of the museum. Why wasn't she an owner?

Right before my eyelids drooped shut, I decided to call and see if I could do an interview with her. As a writer and successful author, I could tell her I was working on a new book and, with her being one of the founding families of

St. Augustine, I needed her unique perspective of the oldest city in the United States.

That was an idea that would come back and bite me in the fanny.

Chapter 4

"**No.**" Vykky was short when I called and asked for an interview. Although I am a wimp in person, I can be very assertive, okay, maybe aggressive, on the phone.

"Ms. deBurgo, since your family was one of the founding members of St. Augustine..."

She interrupted me. "What part of no do you not understand?"

I grinned. I had her now. As long as she stayed on the phone, I had a pretty good chance of getting her to see me.

"You know, we can do a Zoom meeting where we don't actually have to meet in person." I was being coy, "Unless, of course, you're not that familiar with Zoom."

"I certainly do know how to use Zoom," she snapped. "I use it all the time for various meetings."

"Great! Are afternoons or mornings better for you?" I was mentally high fiving myself. I was using the old tried and true sales method of using the assumptive close technique. The person has to make a choice and you're leading them to the close.

"Ms. whatever your name is, I see what you're doing, and it won't work with me." She sounded triumphant.

"Great! I'll see you at the Old Café at ten a.m." I disconnected the call laughing. She wanted to be in charge, I got that. I also guessed that she would show up simply to see who had the audacity to manipulate her into doing so.

I spent the next couple of hours researching her on Google and ended up calling Ronnie for the information that couldn't be found on the internet; specifically, what was her personality really like.

"For that type of information, Miss Harper Rogers, I'm going to need a grande double espresso butter pecan coffee." I could hear the laughter in Ronnie's voice.

"I'll be there in about twenty. Anything else?" I was trying to be accommodating.

Food and coffee were the fastest and simplest ways of getting the scoop on anyone from Ronnie.

"There's a new puppy you can play with, honey. See you!" He disconnected with a lilting laugh.

Doing a slide-and-glide through the local coffee drive-thru, I was at the pet store in record time. I didn't even spill any coffee in the car. I'm prone to do that on occasion.

Doing a Zumba hip move with ease to open the pet store door, I wondered why I couldn't do it in class without creating undue pain in my lower back and down my legs. Life wasn't fair and it was unkind to me in the area of exercise and balance. I've been known to smack into doors quite unintentionally.

Scooping the coffee out of my left hand and replacing it with a sleepy Maltese puppy, Ronnie almost started slurping the coffee before I realized what was going on.

"I so needed this today, honey! Thank you, thank you, thank you!"

Curiosity will override anything else going on in my life. I could wait to ask questions about Miss Vykky.

Snuggling the sleepy puppy closer to my chest while juggling my coffee, "What's going on, Ronnie?"

"You'll never guess who called me asking about you?"

Okay, this was never a good thing when someone wanted to know more about me. I didn't want, need, or even desire to have a stalker in my life. I really just wanted to be left alone and write; well, except I did need to be around people from time to time to help keep me sane. Although that last point may be debatable among certain people. Of course, these people were not my tribe, my peeps, or whatever the phrase-of-the-moment happened to be for people I didn't want anywhere near me.

My mental rolodex was spinning like crazy trying to figure out who could possibly want information about me. I am actually a boring person. I like to write, I'm borderline obsessive about it. I'm a workaholic. I have fun. Maybe not your definition of having fun but you're you and I'm me.

All of these thoughts were shooting at the speed of light through whatever dimensions my brain operated in.

"Vykky deBurgo!" Ronnie was gleeful. I'm not quite sure why but he was.

"Yes, and…" I was cautious, not about Ronnie but about what Vykky wanted to know. As much of a gadabout as Ronnie was, he was very discreet when it came to dispersing gossip and details. I trusted Ronnie.

"She wanted to know who you were, what you were working on, and who you were related to in St. Augustine. I told her you were a bestselling author. I knew you were working on a pirate book, that seemed to really pique her interest, and that you weren't related to anyone in St. Augustine."

Okay, that was all good and it also meant she would meet with me tomorrow morning.

"What else did she say or want to know?" It would be interesting to see what else she wanted to know.

"That was it except that she was meeting you tomorrow morning for coffee." Ronnie giggled, "She did say she didn't appreciate how you manipulated her into doing that except that she'd give you brownie points for your technique."

I told him how I'd done it and we both got a laugh out of it.

"What's the scuttlebutt on her? What's her personality like? Details, Ronnie, details." I looked over the lip of the Styrofoam coffee container.

"Normally, I'd say she's not someone you want to have coffee with but, obviously, you are." He laughed. "She's a little paranoid about people knowing what type of businesses she's involved in. She does loan money to small businesspeople but takes a huge position in their company."

"She's a loan shark."

"Honey, I wouldn't call her that. She's more like a naughty, greedy venture capitalist. To be fair, she does know how to pick winners. The sad part is the business owner is usually desperate for the influx of money and will agree to her terms, which is very advantageous for her and not so much for them."

"Rumors, Ronnie, I want the rumors."

He sighed. "Okay, but you didn't hear it from me. Rumor is she's been looking for a map of buried treasure in St. Augustine where Captain Kidd allegedly hid it.

"It's been heavily rumored for years that John Jacob Astor found the treasure and that's how he got his start in business. He ended up being the first multi-millionaire in the United States."

Ronnie paused, taking another drink of his grande double espresso butter pecan coffee. "Vykky's quite convinced that Captain Kidd's treasure still exists and has never been found. Kidd left a series of numbers or coordinates to his wife that may or may not have been directions to the treasure. That's the reason why she invests so heavily in pirate-related hunts. Regardless of what's found out in the ocean, everything seems to bring treasure hunters back to St. Augustine."

I chuckled. "Well, there's so much history here and I would think the treasure or map or whatever it is would have disappeared a long time ago or, at the very least, still be buried. St. Augustine has a ton of archaeological digs going on at any given time and it seems like something new is discovered every couple of months or so."

Ronnie pranced around the puppies playing with them. "Drake was here before the Old Fort was built. What if the map was buried under the fort?"

We chatted for a few more minutes and then I left. Something was flitting in and out of my brain. It was probably just a butterfly let loose and hadn't discovered its way out yet.

The next morning, I was sitting in the coffee shop waiting on Vykky when it occurred to me I really didn't know what she looked like. As is the case with many women, she changed her hair color and style frequently based on the photos I had seen on Google. A tall, thin woman with black hair pulled back in a severe bun swept into the coffee shop with all of the energy of Attila the Hun. To say this woman was intense was like saying jackhammers don't shatter concrete sidewalks.

Her eyes raked the room, missing nothing. I could feel the blood draining from my heart, I glanced down at my feet to make sure blood wasn't pooling around my toes.

I felt like shooting Ronnie for not telling me her energy level was like that of the space shuttle blasting off from Cape Canaveral.

Virtually, every nerve in my body was shriveling up as her piercing eyes landed on me. Laser-focused, she headed right for my table.

I vaguely wondered if, by osmosis, I could capture some of that energy and bottle it for those days when I felt wimpy...like right now.

Standing up, I held out my hand. She ignored it as she sat down across from me. "Black Americano."

Blinking my eyes several times, I wasn't sure if she was telling me to get her a coffee or was trying to insult me since my skin is a porcelain shade of white or if the coffee shop personnel were being commanded to bring her a cup of the dark brew.

"Do what?" Let me be the first to admit, my brain cells don't always fire on all cylinders particularly when I am exceptionally nervous, which I was.

She waved her hand dismissively at me. "Not you, them."

Attitude, she was all about attitude, with a dash of a sense of entitlement. Considering that her family was one of the founding members of St. Augustine and still owned a great deal of land downtown, maybe she just felt everything was owed to her. In a literal sense, she was right because the store and building owners were paying her rent for their businesses on her property.

Her eyes bore into mine. I think dead shark eyes have more personality. It was like looking into a dark black vortex where there was no bottom. She must have had a vacuum in there somewhere because I could feel myself being sucked into her world and into the hole. It was the strangest of feelings. I was here physically but felt like I was on a highway speeding to an unknown destination.

I blinked my eyes and that broke whatever spell I was under. It jolted me back to looking at Vykky. Her eyes were dark brown. She either had great youthful genes in her DNA or she'd had plastic surgery done. I was betting on plastic surgery.

To say that her makeup was professionally done was an understatement. It looked fabulous. I was actually a little envious. I could spend twenty minutes putting on makeup and it still gave the appearance of either someone who didn't care about their looks, I sort of do, or the artistic skills of a pre-pubescent female teenager. I couldn't even brag that my skills were better than a mortician's, sad to say.

Vykky could be anywhere from thirty-five to seventy-five. Based on what Ronnie had told me and what I was able to glean from Google, she was probably in the neighborhood of a very youthful sixty.

"I normally don't do this type of thing." She was haughty.

For some unknown reason, uncontained and unfiltered words burst out of my mouth and into the atmosphere at the speed of light. "What? You don't have coffee with anyone who's not on the social register?"

Her eyes flashed so quickly I almost missed it, but I thought I saw a spark of amusement. Maybe she wanted to be called out. Maybe she was tired of people kowtowing and appreciated a brief moment of spontaneity from someone who wasn't worth a million dollars or more.

One of the staff brought over her coffee in a delicate white China teacup with a saucer and placed it gently on the table. My coffee was in a cardboard-type cup with a plastic lid. The rich do live in a different world.

"What do you want?" She got right to the point, I had to give her credit for that. She took a sip from the cup.

Throwing all caution to the wind, I plunged ahead hoping she wasn't going to stomp out of the shop. "You're the richest woman in St. Augustine. You are an angel patron to many people and a venture capitalist to business owners."

She merely blinked her eyes and sat the cup back down in the saucer. Her fingertips were lightly resting on the table.

"You also believe Captain Kidd's treasure is still somewhere here in St. Augustine and you want it." I paused, hoping air had somehow magically managed to find its way into my lungs and inflate them so I could breathe without fainting. I was nervous.

She tapped her manicured first fingernail on the table. I couldn't tell if she was annoyed or thinking. I did have the sense not to say anything further. He who speaks first loses is an age-old sales technique. It also usually worked for me in interviews. Most people can't stand the silence after ten to twenty seconds. The longest I've ever had anyone go was thirty seconds before breaking down and answering my questions.

"What's your book about?" Her voice was flat with a slightly curious tinge to it.

"I write murder mysteries and…"

"You want to know if I had anything to do with the murder of George Cloise." She took another sip of coffee.

That thought really had not crossed my mind but now that she had planted it, I was going to run with it.

"Maybe," I was hesitating just enough to pique her interest, "but I'm not investigating his murder."

A slight smile creased her face. I guess she hadn't gone for the Botox treatments because her facial muscles did move.

"You probably should since you're being charged with it."

Chapter 5

News travels fast in the northeast Florida Bermuda Triangle - Jacksonville, St. Augustine, and Palm Park.

I just blinked at her. On any other person, her smile would be a smirk; however, a shark devouring its prey is what popped into my mind.

Lifting her cup to her mouth, she said, "If I'm not mistaken, you weren't supposed to leave Palm Park, yet here you are."

Much as I hated to admit it, she was right...and I knew it. I hoped Sam or one of his buddies in blue didn't suddenly pop through the door and drag me back to Palm Park. My logical mind told me the chances of that happening were between slim and none, and Slim had gone to the Bahamas.

Setting her cup down, "I don't think you have any clue as to what George was doing, what he had, or even what he knew."

She tilted her head to the left slightly. "George was a very unique character who had great contacts in the treasure-hunting field. He knew everyone and, yes, he was on some major finds."

I was watching her body language. She was poised, elegant, and relaxed as a hoot owl getting ready to swoop down and grab a frightened mouse for dinner.

I was the mouse. I was already tense. My stomach needed antacids for the Spanish flotilla swimming around in my belly.

Debating whether to tell her about the person who had tossed the knife at me, I really thought she probably already knew and was playing with me, trying to mess with my psyche. She was doing a fine job of it. I decided not to mention it.

Taking a deep breath, I said, "Tell me…tell me your version." I smiled and hoped my lips weren't trembling as a dead giveaway as to how nervous I was. I held my breath knowing that sooner or later she would tell me something.

"George has something of mine," she paused, taking a tiny sip from her cup, "or, at the very least, knows where it is."

Something suddenly clicked in my brain. "Was George getting Spanish artifacts for either your private collection or for you to sell to a high-end collector?"

Her eyes narrowed. As many times as I've watched snake shows on the National Geographic Channel, I don't think I've ever seen a snake's eyes constrict that quickly.

Gathering my courage, I continued, "That's the reason why you've been his patron for so many years. Let me guess, he keeps leading you on, so you'll continue to sponsor him."

Setting her cup down, daintily patting her lips so her lipstick wouldn't smear, she said, "My dear, you certainly have a vivid imagination but, then again, I guess you would since you're a writer."

She stood up, nodded at the barista, and walked out the door.

If I had to guess, I'd say I may have hit a sour note with her. It also occurred to me that I probably needed to get back to Palm Park before she alerted law enforcement that I had left the county and was probably subject to arrest.

Taking the back way home, I did pass several highway patrol troopers but thankfully, they were not interested in me. I was also going just a couple of miles over the speed limit but not enough to raise any suspicions.

My phone rang. "So did you enjoy your trip to St. Augustine this morning?"

Rats! Sam knew, maybe he had a tracker or something on my car but that didn't really make any sense.

"Did you want to go for coffee or is this call for something else?" I tried very hard to sound cheerful.

He sighed. "Harper, seriously, don't leave the county. If…"

"Sam, I'm not under arrest and I'm pretty sure I can go wherever I want."

There was a long pause. "Harper, when a law enforcement officer asks you not to leave the county, did you think that was a guideline for other people?"

I couldn't help it, I giggled. "How did you know I left the county?"

"The person you met with for coffee has a lot of contacts and a lot of pull, Harper. That individual has also let it be known that you are casting dispersions on her character. She's also let it be known that if you continue to do that, she might be inclined to file a lawsuit against you."

Now, I burst into outright laughter. "Are you serious, Sam? We were having a private conversation, no one was close by, and our entire meeting was probably no longer than fifteen minutes. If she is threatening a lawsuit over something this frivolous, then she's got something to hid. The question is what.

"By the way, she said I was under arrest and I'm not, am I?"

"Not at the moment. You don't want to swim with the sharks, Harper. Have a great day."

The call was disconnected. I looked at my phone and shook my head. I think Sam was trying to warn me about Miss Vykky but for what purpose I wasn't exactly sure.

Deciding Ronnie probably had the answer for this, I did a slide and glide through the coffee drive-thru and got two coffees and four doughnuts.

Ronnie's such a ray of sunshine and I appreciate his friendship. He's always so happy to see me when I come through the pet store door especially when I'm bearing gifts.

"Oh, honey, look at what you've brought me! You are so sweet! I love, love, love you, honey!" He was doing air kisses while gently easing one of the coffees from my hand to his.

As he was nibbling on the doughnut between sips of coffee, I told him everything that had happened.

"So, do you think Vykky had George killed?"

"Well, here's the thing, Ronnie. She didn't get upset until I basically implied that he was blackmailing her."

"That would do it, honey," he took another sip. "Particularly, since you insulted her intelligence and…"

"Whoa! Wait up right there, Ronnie! I never said the woman was dumb or stupid."

He waved his hand at me as little sugar flecks fell off his doughnut. "You told her that George was leading her on and that's the reason why she continued to be his patron. That's saying she wasn't smart enough to find out what he had, and she was paying for the privilege of being stupid."

Crap doodle! I hadn't even thought of that. It never occurred to me that what I meant could be misconstrued that way. If I wrote that scene in a book, I would have caught it but being in real life, words have a nasty way of causing me all sorts of problems. Things that simply would never occur to me normally. Maybe there is something wrong with my brain. Whatever filters had been given to most people apparently were rather scarce in my brain.

"Honey, don't worry about it. I love you anyway." Ronnie stood up and gave me a platonic hug. "However, it does sound like you may have stepped on Vykky's toes and that's probably not a good thing."

We chatted for a few more minutes and I went home, had an early dinner, and was just getting ready for my shower when my doorbell rang. I looked through the peephole and saw Sam. Grinning, I opened the door.

"Harper Rogers, did you threaten to murder Vykky deBurgo?"

Chapter 6

"**No**," **I stuttered. My brain** was swirling. What was going on? Was Vykky threatening me to leave her alone with some bogus, trumped-up charge?

I think I started hyperventilating because I do remember Sam sitting me down on the couch and handing me a paper bag. I didn't realize I had one in the house or maybe he just always carried one when he was the bearer of bad news.

"Am I being arrested?" I huffed out trying to catch my breath. I was sure my brain had been deprived of oxygen. Nothing was making any sense.

"No," he paused, "Not at this time. Do you want me to get you a Coke or something to drink?"

"Why...why...," I took a deep breath, "why are you here then?"

Sam squirmed, cracked his knuckles, and looked uncomfortable. "You realize that there are certain things in life one must do to appease the higher ups, right?"

My mind snapped back into gear. Oxygen flooded into my lungs and rejuvenated my blood cells so I could think clearly. I was no longer spinning like a Jewish dreidel at Christmas time. I hissed, "You were told to come over here and threatened or intimidate me to leave Vykky alone? You do realize I only spoke to her on the phone once and met her in person for about fifteen minutes, right?"

He shifted and couldn't seem to get comfortable on my sofa. Sam wouldn't look at me. This meant he was being forced to do something he disagreed with or that he knew had zero merit and that it was a complete waste of time.

"So, this is her method of intimidation? To get local police to warn me to leave her alone?" I snarled, setting the brown paper bag aside. "One would think you have something better to do than this, Sam."

He almost squirmed on the couch and looked away. What kind of detective was Sam if he was this uncomfortable answering my questions? I'm going to go with it was probably because we were friends, and he didn't like this aspect of his job.

He suddenly stood up. "Harper, this is as a friend," Ha! I was right. "You don't want to mess with Miss duBorg."

I pointed to the door. "You can tell your superiors I am not easily intimidated. Oh, yeah, ask them why they're giving warnings for someone who doesn't even live in our county."

On a roll, I continued, "You do realize this is like Mafia tactics, don't you?"

He shook his head, exhaled deeply, opened the door, and said, "I'm just saying, Harper, be careful. She's got a lot of tentacles and you don't want to be caught up in them."

I shut the door a little harder than I meant to...sorry, I lied. I really meant to slam it but I didn't whip my arm back far enough to slam it like a cat five hurricane attack.

I called A.B.'s office and told her what had happened. Her only response was, "That's interesting. Keep working on your book."

Probably good advice but things kept whirling around in my mind. Had I inadvertently stumbled onto something that Vykky didn't want me to find out about? She was definitely warning me away. I'd like to tell her 'foolish woman' but I had better sense. I don't think this had to do with my inadvertent suggestion that she had been played by George.

I needed to do more research on George. I wondered if he had any other patrons for his business or treasure-hunting expeditions.

After several hours of going down the Google rabbit hole on George, his treasure-hunting expeditions, and then turning my attention to the ever-curious Vykky. She's to the point of massive intrigue for me. She's revved up my curiosity level. Before she was only mildly interesting, now I want to know what makes her tick. Once I know that, I can either annoy her greatly or figure out a way to make her neuroses work for me. Of course, I was now borderline paranoid about everything.

My phone started playing. I picked up without looking at the caller I.D. I thought it was Ronnie calling me. I was wrong.

I answered the answer without the butterflies in my stomach flying in unison. I hoped my voice didn't sound as shaky as it felt.

"Hello."

"You really don't want to mess with me." The call disconnected. What did the caller I.D. say? Vykky duBorg. Shut the front door!

Chapter 7

That was certainly something I wasn't expecting. At least, I was able to keep breathing at this point. That's progress.

My nerves were shot. Vykky's call sounded like a threat. I called my attorney who was now not only on speed dial but I had also memorized her number in case my phone was ever taken from me.

"A.B., what does that mean for me?" I'm not going to lie, I was scared. "Um, if I were thinking out loud, should I plan on moving to Costa Rica or the Virgin Islands?"

She ignored my question. "Don't worry about Vykky unless she starts making five or more calls in a day and then we can file harassment charges against her."

Disconnecting my phone, it rang again almost immediately. The good news was it interrupted the downward spiral of negative thoughts that were threatening to overtake my brain and causing it to shut down.

"Honey, what is going on with you?" Ronnie sounded a little distraught. "I'm bringing pizza over."

There's always time for pizza. Ronnie was my BFF and was so incredibly thoughtful. Every girl should have a guy friend like Ronnie.

I had two Cokes waiting when I heard the tapping at my door. Call me gun shy but I did look through the peephole to make sure it was him and not Sam coming to deliver another nasty message from his superiors again.

Opening the door, Ronnie borderline pranced in. "I got the PMS special!" He announced gleefully.

Shaking my head, "Only you call it that. It's pepperoni, mushrooms, and sausage to most normal people."

"Oh, honey, that ship normal sailed a long time ago." We both giggled.

Chowing down on the pizza, I caught him up with everything that had happened and ended with, "Nothing is making any sense."

"What does A.B. say about all of this?"

Shrugging, "Not much. She told me to ignore Vykky unless she starts blowing up my phone. By the way, who did the interior design in her office? I absolutely love it!"

"Some gal out of Atlanta." Taking a big gulp of his Coke, "Don't worry about a thing, A.B. will take good care of you. I think Vykky doesn't like you."

I snorted. "Ya think? I'm wondering if I should retaliate against her."

Ronnie looked up, his eyeballs peeking over the top of his glasses. "Seriously, Harper Elizabeth Rogers, that is not one of your better ideas. You're already being investigated for murder. Adding another one to your list of things to do will not, repeat will not, help you in a court of law. Don't even think about writing it down as a book idea."

Wiping his mouth, "All of this being said, I think Vykky thinks you know something about Captain Kidd's treasure. She's going to put enough pressure on you to make you cough up Anne Bonny and Mary Read!"

"Who never came to St. Augustine!" I grabbed another slice of pizza. "What do you think happened to Kidd's treasure?"

He grinned, "I think it's already been found and different parts of it have already been sold to high-end collectors. That being said, I don't think the majority of it has been dispersed. I think whoever found it wants to keep it in that one location."

"Gives a whole new meaning to pirate booty, doesn't it?" I laughed. "But there's a whole school of thought that says the treasure is over in South Africa somewhere or maybe that was Sir Francis Drake. I get the two of them confused."

Ronnie wiggled his eyebrows at me. "See? That's half the fun of trying to figure out where pirate treasure is supposed to be buried. I honestly don't think it's about the actual worth, the dollar figure, of the treasure. I think it's more about discovering what no one else has been able to find. I think that's the juice that drives treasure hunters."

I needed to give A.B. another check just to make sure she was at my beck and call in case those folks dressed in blue with shiny badges decided I needed to be re-introduced to their facility.

Bopping through A.B.'s office doors, I had the good sense to bring doughnuts for Brenda who barely acknowledged my existence. She simply pointed at the inner sanctum doors for me to enter.

A.B. wasn't at her desk when I entered. Since her office was designed in pirate girl décor, I started to wander around the room. She had vibrant colored paintings of various female seafaring entrepreneurs hanging on the walls with a framed placard detailing their escapades. A couple of them had maps underneath the portraits with the always popular 'X marks the spot' on them. I guess pirates all went to the same school of name it and claim it on their buried treasure maps.

She entered through a hidden door I hadn't noticed before. She was grinning. "You really like my office, don't you?"

Smiling, "I think it's a great testimony to female pirates, certainly to the power of women, and I love how you have the treasure maps next to everyone's painting."

Looking around, I said, "Captain Kidd is the only male pirate you have in your office."

"Oh, that," she waved her hand and semi-laughed, "theoretically, his daughter is my great, great, umpteen greats grandmother."

I was fascinated by that. "Really? That's cool. Um, I thought Vykky might be related to him and that's the reason why she has the hots for buried treasure."

A.B. smiled, "Vykky couldn't find Kidd's treasure if it came up and bit her on her Botoxed face."

Meow! I wondered if there was something between Vykky and A.B. I started to ask but A.B. started discussing my case with me and I forgot. I'm easily distracted, what can I say?

Leaving her office, I was encouraged that nothing was going to happen to me. I wasn't going to go to jail. I wasn't going to have to wear orange. I don't know what strings she pulled or what favors she called in, but I was free to roam the Northeast Florida Bermuda Triangle and

I could go to St. Augustine any time I wanted. I was a free woman.

I had no sooner gotten home than my phone rang. I didn't look at caller I.D., I probably should have.

"Yo, what's up?" I really thought it was Ronnie. I couldn't have been any more wrong.

It was Vykky.

Chapter 8

I gulped and then flattened my voice. I certainly wasn't happy to hear from her. She had caused me a great deal of grief and aggravation.

"Yes, Vykky, what do you want?"

Her voice was well-modulated. "I'd like to know how you managed to use a get out of jail free card."

I couldn't help myself. "I passed go and collected two hundred dollars."

Assuming I had annoyed her greatly because it took a moment or two for her to say anything. "Who's your attorney?"

"Nunya."

"Nunya," she repeated slowly, "what does that mean?"

"None of your business." I disconnected the call and blocked her.

Why do I fascinate this odd woman? Now I was more determined than ever to find out what the connection was with George and this socialite businesswoman. There had to be more than just Vykky financially sponsoring him. It occurred to me that he was blackmailing her. If that were true, what did he have on her that was worth his death? More importantly, chances were, she didn't have it in her possession. She obviously either thought I had it or knew what it was.

What was I wearing that day? Did George slip something in my pocket or purse that day unbeknownst to me?

I wasn't sure which purse I was carrying that day because I frequently changed them. I usually only pulled my wallet out of one purse and put it in another one. I typically didn't see what else was in the purse.

Going into my small closet, I pulled the straw tote out and turned it upside down on my bed. I didn't see anything in the contents that looked unusual – a handful of tissues, a ballpoint pen, a band-aid, and three single dollar bills. I was rich!

Putting everything back in the tote, I placed it back on the closet shelf. Grabbing the black purse, I dumped everything on the bed. How in the heck did I get dust bunnies in my purse? That didn't make sense and I usually kept my purses zipped up when I wasn't using them. This time, the bag was unzipped. The little dust bunnies looked like tiny little cotton buds that had escaped from the end of a Q-tip. There were six of them laying on top of my tissues, a band-aid, yes I carry band-aids in all of my purses in case I suffer a painful papercut during my travels, and my sunglasses. I wondered where I had lost them. Other than the weird dust bunnies, nothing seemed to be unusual.

I only had one other purse to peruse and that was the current one I was using. I turned it upside down on the bed cover, a little piece of paper floated out and laid on top of the tissues, band-aid, and my wallet. It looked like a Chinese fortune cookie message except there wasn't a printed message. It was a handwritten note with 29°53′41″N, 81°18′52″W scrawled on it.

After plugging that into Google, it only came up as St. Augustine. Well, that wasn't particularly helpful. St. Augustine sprawled almost eleven square miles where roughly eight and a half miles was land, and the remaining two and a half miles was water. It did occur to me that Kidd's treasure might be in the Inland Waterway or that when it was being dredged umpteen years ago, the construction crew had already found the treasure, divvied it up, and spent it. I didn't think so, but you never know.

Deciding this might be something A.B. needed to know, I called her office, told Brenda I needed to speak to her, and the soul of brevity put me through.

"What's going on, Harper?" A.B. always sounded happy to talk to me, despite her seeing me several hours earlier.

I told her about the little piece of paper with the latitude and longitude written. She asked me what it specifically said and the only response I received was, "Humm, that's interesting."

"Why?" I was curious.

"If I remember correctly, I think that's really close to some property Vykky owns."

Yes, I thought it beyond interesting that my attorney would know the latitude and longitude of any piece of property anywhere much less that it was close to property Vykky owned.

"A.B., are you related to Vykky by any chance?"

She laughed. "That's an amusing thought, probably more to you than me or Vykky."

Was this a non-denial denial or just the basic I'm-not-answering-any-questions attorney jargon?

"Bring it down the next time you come this way. Put it somewhere out of sight though."

"So, it might be important then?"

"Who knows? Maybe but probably not."

We rang off.

It was time for me to visit Ronnie. I had a ton of questions. If anyone would know, it would probably be Ronnie.

Yes, I was going to bribe him with doughnuts and coffee. I'm surprised neither one of us was obese from the amount of caffeine and sugar we consumed on a weekly basis.

"Ronnie," I singsonged entering the Furever Love Palace, "guess what I have."

Zooming from the back of the pet store to the front, I was surprised the man had never tried out for the one-hundred-meter dash in the Olympics.

He snatched the Brazilian coffee out of my hands and took a big gulp before I had the opportunity to warn him it was different from butter pecan and was exceptionally hot. He almost gagged and

I could almost see his eyeballs spinning around with the extra caffeine.

"Honey, honey," he sputtered, "are you trying to kill me?"

I was bent over with laughter. "If you would have waited for a couple of seconds, I would have told you it was something different."

"This is rocket fuel," he choked out. "What are you trying to find out today by bringing this to me?"

"Is A.B. related to Vykky in some way?"

Shaking his head, "I don't know. I don't think so but, then again, Vykky doesn't admit to being related to anyone other than her mother and father and the founders of St. Augustine. I'm not even sure if she has any brothers or sisters. If she does, I'm sure they don't live in St. Augustine."

Taking a small sip of his high-octane caffeine fuel, "I simply don't ever remember hearing about her having any siblings. Maybe her mom and dad decided she was perfect enough, they couldn't do any better, and they stopped making babies."

I had picked up one of the little fluffy balls of Maltese love and told him about the note in my purse. "Don't you think it's odd that A.B. would know the latitude and longitude of St. Augustine?"

"Nope." He opened the doughnut bag and pulled the glazed yeast deliciousness out. "Remember, A.B. blew out the SAT test for the state of Florida when she was a senior and you were a sophomore. That perfect score had never happened before and has never occurred since. It caused all those academic types to wonder what they did wrong and how a high school senior could score perfectly on their test.

"The woman remembers all sorts of things. I think she told me once she has an eidetic memory. She sees it once and it is set for life in her brain."

A.B. was brilliant and I was happy to have her as my attorney.

"Ronnie, why is she practicing law here instead of some big law firm in a large city?"

He laughed, "Because she can work when she wants to. You do know that she came up with and patented Scrubby Bubbles, right?"

I shook my head.

"Yeah, about eight years ago she appeared on Shark Tank and one of the sharks wanted to buy the entire company for something like a million dollars. A.B. retained a three percent share, smuck insurance as she called it, and sold the company to the shark. Then four years ago, the shark sold it for seventy-five million dollars and her three percent share ended up being something like two point two five million dollars. A.B. doesn't have to work unless she just wants to."

Oh.

We chatted for a few more minutes and I headed home where I discovered Sam waiting by my door with a pizza in his hand.

How much pizza can a girl eat in a day?

Chapter 9

I almost fainted. I felt like I was in the wind tunnel of a tornado. I was Dorothy in the Wizard of Oz, and I hadn't been smacked in the head with a flying window from a Kansas tornado. Taking a deep breath, I noticed Sam had placed his hand in the middle of my back. I was assuming it was because if I did faint, it would make it easier for him to guide me down to the floor.

"What are you doing here, Sam?" I managed to take a deep breath. "Are you coming to give me another warning from your head honchos?"

Unlocking the door, we walked in. He put the pizza on the countertop and took a couple of glasses down from the cupboard. Placing them under the ice cube dispenser, he filled the glasses up. Unscrewing the top from the large Coke bottle I had sitting on the counter, I waited until it quit hissing and poured it over the ice. The crinkling sound of the cubes gave me a few more minutes so I could gather my thoughts.

Smiling so that his dimples showed, "It's a peace offering, Harper. I'm on my own time and not police time."

I snorted, "I thought cops were always on duty."

"I'm a detective, remember?" His smile was still there. "And, no, I'm not always looking for criminals. It wasn't fair for me to do that the other day and I apologize."

My little radar was going ninety-to-nothing wondering what the real purpose of his visit was. I'd like to think it's because he likes me and we're friends. The suspicious part of me didn't believe he was only here because we were friends in the slightest.

"What? You look like you don't…" His smile widened.

"I'm not buying what you're selling." I was trying to sound firm when I was getting little vibrations throughout my body. There are days I'd like for us to be more than friends, but this wasn't that day. Maybe. Nope, nope, nope, I had to remind myself to stay firm in my resolve not to drop my guard against a bona fide detective.

"Um, Sam, does Vykky duBorg have a sister or any other relatives that you know of?" I started nibbling on a slice of pepperoni pizza.

"You know, I'm not sure." He took a swig of his Coke. "I had heard at one time, and this was a bazillion years ago, and…"

I couldn't help it, I started to laugh. "Bazillion?"

Sam looked puzzled and did a semi-shrug. "I don't understand."

"Really? You used the word bazillion." I continued to laugh and tried not to choke on my slice, "Who knew that you would ever use that word?"

He started to laugh. "It's as good a redneck word as any."

The little bit of tension in the air dissipated. Because I can be annoyingly focused...or so I've been told...I asked him again, "Does her Royal Highness Vykky have any siblings or cousins or anything?"

"Oh, yeah, back to that, huh?" He took another sip of his Coke. "I had heard years ago that her mother had a sister, but she didn't live in Florida."

He shrugged, "That's all I got and I'm not even sure that's true. All of this was," he grinned again, "a bazillion years ago."

We laughed again and chatted about nothing. I didn't tell him about Vykky calling me. For the time being, I wanted to keep my cards close to my vest. I didn't think he was a wolf in sheep's clothing this go-round but, still, I was a wee bit cautious.

I decided to step out on a limb. "Sam, what do you think this whole thing is about with Vykky?"

He lifted his shoulders and dropped them. "Other than the fact you've really riled her up, I don't have a clue."

Grinning, "Maybe, in your research, you've stumbled onto something about her or something that she wants, and you just don't know it."

"The only thing I've been researching are pirates. I wasn't even interested in their treasure. I'm predominantly interested in their clothing, what their eating utensils were, and their weapons." I sighed, "I can't imagine how cranky they must have been in those heavy clothes in Florida's heat and humidity."

"You're not interested in their treasure?" Sam was incredulous.

I shook my head. "You can look up clothes and everything online but until you see how heavy the clothes were, it really doesn't register."

"No treasure?" Sam was still shocked.

"No. Honestly, Sam, that's it. I was just doing research. I'm not one for digging around in the dirt or going underwater to find treasure. Let someone else do it. Remember, I work really hard on this porcelain white skin. I don't like to be out in the sun all that much."

"Living room light bulb tan then, huh?" We both laughed.

My phone pinged. "Hold on a second, my attorney is calling me."

At least he was a gentleman, "I'll step out into the hallway to give you some privacy."

"Hi, A.B., what's up?"

"Is anyone with you?" Her voice sounded very happy.

"Well, Sam came over, brought pizza, and now he's stepped out into the hallway."

She laughed, "Are you two dating?"

I sighed and rolled my eyes. "It's more like friends with no benefits."

Chuckling, "I understand. Okay, I've been able to see the video from the Pirate Museum and you're completely in the clear."

I sat down on the sofa and felt like the weight of the world had been lifted from my shoulders. No longer was I Atlas, the mythological god banished to carrying the world on his shoulders.

"Wha...what does it show?" I was anxious and curious at the same time.

"There was a guy behind George with a ball cap on. He was very careful to make sure his face was never shown from the time he entered the Pirate Museum lobby to actually going in the museum and then his hasty exit."

Yes, she really does talk like that.

"And..."

A.B. continued, "It appears that he stabbed George in the back and as George was turning, he stabbed him again. It is very clear in the video that your back was to George when all of this was occurring. You didn't turn around until the assailant tossed the knife at you and then you promptly dropped it." She paused for a moment, "Because you never actually caught it to begin with."

She started to laugh. "Harper, if I remember correctly from high school, you have absolutely no athletic coordination skills whatsoever, do you?"

As embarrassing as it was, I have to admit it's still as true today as it was during my high school years. I nodded my head and then realizing A.B. couldn't see me doing that answered with a pitiful sounding, "No, I don't."

"That totally lets you off the hook for the murder of George Cloises."

"What happened to the guy that murdered him?" I couldn't recall a single thing about the man.

"He ran out the Employees Only door."

Taking a deep breath, I let it out slowly. "Let me guess, there's no cameras in there and there's probably not any outside either, right?"

"Bingo."

"So, A.B., does that mean he got away with murder?" Wild thoughts were dashing around in my head equivalent to the spin cycle on a washing machine. I was a little apprehensive. "Do I have to worry about him coming to get me?"

"Probably not, Harper. I think you were a person of opportunity for him."

"A.B., last thing, what do you think this is all about?"

"Not enough information to make a guess at this point, Harper. Have a great day."

Relief was an understatement. I almost bounced over to the door to let Sam back in.

He saw me grinning like the proverbial Cheshire cat. "I take it everything's good."

"Yes!" I looked him directly in the eye. "Did you know the video shows me with my back to George?"

His eyes widened, okay, so he didn't know. "No, I didn't know that. How did your attorney get the tape and we didn't?"

Interesting choice of words. I was smug, "Probably because it happened in St. Johns County where you don't have any jurisdiction and not here in River County."

He nodded, looking thoughtful. Okay, I opened a can of worms on that but, realistically, he didn't have any jurisdiction for the St. Augustine area, and I doubted they'd share the information with him or even his supervisors. Law enforcement likes to keep things to their own agency so they can receive all the glory in the news media when they solve a crime.

Looking at me, "Mind if I make a quick phone call?"

I didn't think it made any difference what I told him, he was going to do it anyway.

"As long as I can listen in." I smiled sweetly. It's my apartment and I didn't want to go stand in the hallway.

"Sure." He punched in some numbers, glanced at me, and said, "Hey, it's Sam. What do you have on the video of Harper Rogers and George Cloises at the Pirate Museum?" A couple of ums and hums then, "Okay, thanks."

With raised eyebrows, I looked at him.

"How did your attorney get the Pirate Museum videotape? St. Augustine PD hasn't seen it yet."

Chapter 10

"You really should back off if you know what's good for you."

Vykky looked at her phone with the blocked number. Her eyes narrowed. How had someone gotten her personal phone number? She always used her other phone for everything related to business. Very few people had this number.

"What..."

The caller had already disconnected. Vykky's jaw tightened. Murmuring to herself, "Harper, dear, you're going to pay for that."

Chapter 11

"You know, Sam, there are some things in life I don't need to know about. You know, like electricity. I don't care how it's made, just that when I turn on the switch my light comes on."

"Harper..."

I grinned. "Seriously, I have no clue and, no, I'm not going to ask A.B. I can't be charged with anything and if Vykky decides to continue to make my life miserable, I'll just turn everything over to A.B. and let her handle everything."

He wiggled his eyebrows. "I don't think you want to play hardball with her. She's got more money than you and can make your life really miserable."

"True," I agreed, "however, I'm a very small fish to her and I would hazard a guess that she would get tired of me pretty quickly."

He left shortly thereafter, although, he did kiss me on the cheek. That was a surprise, and, yes, it did make me feel all tingly. Maybe there was something there after all. A girl could hope.

Calling Ronnie, I spilled everything to him. It's a good thing he couldn't see me through the phone because I was actually blushing like a schoolgirl from her first kiss.

"Girl, I've told you before, you both have sparks for each other. Just that neither one of you will admit to it." He sighed and almost giggled, "I think I know the two of you better than you know yourself."

At least I was smart enough to realize that he knew me better than I understood myself. Even though I have rampant thoughts merrily tap dancing their way through my brain, I just don't think I'm that personally aware. I'm a writer and I live too much in my brain anyway.

Deciding to sleep in the next day, I was rudely awakened by my phone ringing.

Struggling to become awake and find my phone at the same time was meant for someone who was physically more co-ordinated than I am. I knocked it on the floor. I finally found it under the bed but it had already stopped ringing. Looking through the recent calls, it was A.B.

She could wait until I had coffee. I'm not a very nice person before coffee. If Sam and I ever hooked up, I should probably tell him that.

After I'd had my second coffee, coming awake, and having my brain cells flying somewhat in formation, I returned A.B.'s call. The efficient Brenda did her standard 'let me see if she's available' thing.

It took a moment or two before A.B. came on the line. I could tell she was busy because she got right to the point.

"Harper, the St. Augustine P.D. has I.D.'d the man who murdered George Cloises."

"Wonderful!" I exclaimed. "Has he been arrested?"

"No. They found him in the dumpster behind the Pirate Museum. He's dead.

Looks like he was shot in the forehead with a pirate's gun."

My head was swimming. "What do you mean he was shot with a pirate gun? Don't they make a lot of noise?"

"It was an English flintlock fifty caliber and, yes, they make a fair amount of noise. He was found this morning when one of the employees came to work."

"Whoa, A.B.! What do you think happened?"

"Shear speculation. Whoever hired him to kill George killed him and dumped his body."

"A.B., who was this guy?" I was curious. Did I know him? Was there some weird connection between us? I knew I was in the clear but this was all so very strange.

"Some guy by the name of Todd Stein. Had an arrest record as long as my arm, been in and out of jail since he was a kid, and had only been out of prison for a couple of weeks. Do you know him?"

She caught me off guard. I was going through names in my head. "Um, no, I don't think so. Do you know him, A.B.?"

She sort of laughed. "No, if I did, he wouldn't have spent as much time in jail as he did."

"A.B., don't you think it's weird that he was shot with a pirate gun? Why would someone do that?"

She started to say something when I interrupted her. "Wait, wait! There aren't any cameras by that door, are there? This means someone knew that and it also means someone had access to one of the pirate guns."

She was brisk. "Yes to your first question. Possibly to your second comment. Someone could have had a flintlock pistol in their own home versus taking something out of the museum. No, they don't have a suspect at this time. Talk to you later."

Questions were swirling as I sat at my laptop and started typing. If the guy was in the dumpster, that meant either a hefty person, probably a male, lifted the body up and pushed it into the dumpster after he was shot or someone had this Todd person sit on the edge of the trash container and when he was shot he fell backward into the container. I didn't know anyone who would willingly sit on top of a trash container strongly suspecting their immediate demise.

I googled Todd Stein, found his jail log information, and looked at the ever-popular jailhouse photo – black barber apron around his neck and only his face showing. He looked to be a slim man, maybe in the one forty – one fifty pound range.

Who could lift a man in that weight category? I wondered if I could do it. Pondering on that for a few minutes, it suddenly occurred to me that I probably could if, and only if, he were standing on a box. If he were standing flat-footed, chances were I wouldn't be able to lift a lifeless body into the dumpster.

This begged the next question, were there two people involved?

I was still of the opinion Vykky had something to do with this. I just didn't know how yet. She might not have been there or even shot Todd but, the more I thought about it, the more convinced I was she was behind two murders.

The next question became who was closest to her and had been with her or in her employ for a number of years.

I called Ronnie.

"Hey, honey, I need a coffee. Miss Priss and Mr. Randy Dandy are trying to have conjugal relations and it's really too soon for them to be doing that. I'm stressed, honey!"

Knowing that I probably shouldn't laugh but I did anyway, I agreed to bring him a coffee.

Because I have a whacky sense of humor, I stuck my hand holding the coffee through the store's door.

"Oooo, girl! Thank you!" I heard him squeal. It was safe for me to enter.

"Ronnie, it has…" I never got to finish my sentence because he started sputtering.

"Do you hate me so much that you can't be bothered to tell me what coffee you are bringing me?" He tried to sound upset but was kind of chuckling at the same time. "Does this have espresso in it?"

I was almost doubled over with laughter. "Yes. Ronnie, I was going to tell you but you snatched it out of my hand so quickly I didn't have a chance to tell you."

"You lie!" We both laughed. "Okay, Miss Trying-to-Butter-Me-Up-and-Ask-Questions, what do you need to know now? And I'm guessing it has to do with Vykky."

"Yes, who does she have, a man, who's been with her the longest?"

Ronnie paused and stroked his beard. "Probably Raoul. He's her handyman. He's not much bigger than me but he's incredibly strong."

"Do you think he could lift a hundred and fifty pounds of dead weight from the ground and throw it over his shoulders?"

He nodded. "He could probably do two hundred pounds pretty easily. He used to do all of Vykky's landscaping and gardening. He lifted a lot of mulch, grass pallets, that type of thing."

I thought I was getting close to what had happened to Todd Stein.

"How loyal is he to Vykky?" I held my breath. Ronnie knew everything. I never asked him how or where he got his information. Some things I don't need to know.

"Well, I know she brought his family over from Venezuela a long time ago and bought a house for his mom and sisters. Then a couple of years ago, she bought him the house he was renting. It's about a mile from his mom's house. We were at a club one time with a bunch of other people and he said he would do anything for Vykky because she had saved his family from all of the political upheaval in Venezuela. Apparently, Vykky pulled a few strings and they were able to immigrate here. I think she might have gotten them here by asking they be given political asylum."

Vykky was resourceful, had the money and means to do something like that, and what better way to ensure someone's loyalty forever than by taking care of the one thing they value the most – family.

I told Ronnie what I suspected had happened to Todd Stein.

"Probably so," he agreed, "but, here's the thing, Harper, there's still no motive as to why George was murdered. You're focusing on the wrong thing."

"But, but, another man was killed," I sputtered. I hated to admit that I had been distracted by this new murder and not focusing on the why of George's murder.

Somewhat humbled but refusing to admit it, I asked, "So, what's your theory on why George was killed?"

Ronnie laughed, sounding like a little boy who had just caught a jumping frog. "Harper, you're the one with all the ideas. You go first and then I'll tell you."

Rats! Ronnie had outplayed me once again.

"Honestly, Ronnie, I'm not one hundred percent sure. I think he found or knew of some more Spanish treasure. I'm guessing it was substantial and he was going to sell it to another museum or collectors so he had enough money to buy his way out of Vykky's grasp and she wasn't having it. She probably wanted the treasure and to keep him under her thumb. When he refused to tell her, she had him killed."

Ronnie shook his head. "Nope, not all of that makes any sense. She wasn't about to kill the goose that laid the golden egg."

Rolling my eyes, I demanded "What's your theory then? Remember, stabbing is up close and personal. This wasn't a warning shot she was firing at him."

"I think he did find the map to some treasure, whether or not it was to Captain Kidd's alleged bounty, who knows. But I do think he probably showed her some artifacts or doubloons."

Dubious, I waved my hand at him to continue. Picking up Mr. Randy Dandy, one of the overly exuberant Maltese puppies trying to mate with Miss Priss, he grimaced, "Harper, what am I going to do with these two? They're not old enough to be doing the naughty-naughty."

I laughed and picked up Miss Priss. She snuggled up against my shoulder and cheek. "And..."

"And I'm going to have to keep them separated." He sighed, "What's a daddy to do?"

Rolling my eyes, "Ronnie, focus. What do you think happened?"

Putting Mr. Randy Dandy in his own little playpen and watching the overly excited puppy run around with his tongue hanging out, he sighed and shook his head. He turned back to me, "George found some type of treasure, didn't offer it to Vykky but asked how much would it take to get out of their business deal.

Vykky probably smelled a skunk right from the beginning because she knew George didn't have any money to buy her out.

"That could only mean one thing to her, George had found some pirate treasure, probably a lot of it, or he had found a map or both. Regardless, she was going to be cut out of what she probably thought was a substantial amount of money."

"Okay, that makes sense," I nodded.

Ronnie continued, "I would hazard a guess that Vykky thought she was being double-crossed, wanted the treasure or map, and if she had that, she didn't need George anymore."

Putting Miss Priss in another doggie playpen, I asked, "But why would she kill him if he had all of this information?"

Ronnie smiled, "Because there were only two places George would have kept a map – either on his person or in the cannon barrel. Chances were he'd put it in the barrel."

Snapping my fingers, I exclaimed, "Of course, then whoever murdered him could come back at any time and get the map. Wait! How do you know where George would put a map?"

"Some things, honey, you just don't need to know." Ronnie winked at me. I really didn't need to know the answer. Some things are just better left unknown.

"Except when Todd Stein came back to find the map, it wasn't there," I surmised.

"Probably," he agreed. "Vykky might have thought she was being double-crossed again and had him murdered also."

"And she still doesn't have the map!" We said in unison, high fiving each other.

After giggling for a few minutes, I said, "She's got to be one frustrated woman."

"Probably in more ways than one," grinned Ronnie wiggling his eyebrows. I playfully slapped him.

"Well, I need to get back to work on my murder mystery."

"What's this one about, Harper?" Ronnie was being polite, I knew he was more into movies and the club scene rather than the printed word.

"Originally, it was going to be about the pirates sailing around Florida, looting everything, and murder on the high seas." I shrugged, grinned, and rolled my eyes. "You know, kind of a historical murder mystery. Nothing like what's going on now. I might have to change what I'm writing."

"Naw, keep doing what you're doing."

"Seriously, Ronnie, all I was really doing at the Pirate Museum was looking at the pirate clothing, guns, and anything related to the way they lived their life. My research really had nothing to do with treasure or anything like that. How I ended up being involved in a murder is beyond me."

"Dead bodies do seem to show up around you on a somewhat frequent basis," he said, not looking at me.

I huffed, "I'd like to point out that I never had anything like this happen to me when I lived in Jacksonville. I move back to Palm Park and weird stuff happens. I believe it's something in the water."

I'd had several really unfortunate incidents over the past however many months where people just up and died near me. I didn't commit any of them, I swear it! Did I end up solving the whodunnit factor? Well, yes, and that's how Detective Sam Needles came into my life but that's another story. My brain had probably morphed into Stephen Hawking's black hole theory where things just disappear forever...or, they change into another life form, I don't know. All I do know is I have thoughts circulating in my head that I'm pretty sure other human beings have never had cross their minds.

This whole thing with Vykky was one of the universe's black holes for me. I felt like I was being sucked into another galaxy and there were no answers for anything. It's bad enough I can do this on my own since I'm a writer but to have external forces creating this havoc in my brain really just wasn't acceptable to me. The question became what was I going to do about it?

I left the Furever Love pet store and headed home. The front door opened way too easily. All I did was put my key in the lock and it opened.

If I'd had the sense of a goose, I wouldn't have walked into my own apartment and called the police instead but since, obviously, whatever few precious brain cells I had went the way of a cat playing with a twisted feather boa, I entered my abode and discovered someone had thoughtfully rearranged my carefully feng shui placed furniture.

What's the short version? Some jerk had trashed my apartment. Everything was turned upside down and my sofa looked like it had been shredded by an untrained puppy on some hallucinogenic drug.

I punched Sam's number on my phone. "Hey, do you think you could send someone over here? My place's been completely trashed." My voice was a little shaky. My apartment had been rearranged several times over the past however months and each time it was because of me being involved in solving a murder. I'd like to point out that none of them had attended the Martha Stewart School of Interior Decorating.

The inside of my brain was turning into a ping-pong match of errant thoughts. I think the Chinese were winning at this point.

"Don't touch anything, Harper," ordered Sam. "I'll be right over. I'm assuming you don't have anyone else in the apartment with you."

Um, I hadn't thought to look but I didn't think so. "No."

I did look around my formerly tidy place but I didn't see anyone hiding behind upturned furniture.

Sam showed up ten minutes later. Palm Park is a small town and you can go from one end of town to the other in about fifteen minutes.

He looked stoic. "Harper, have you ever thought about moving back to Jacksonville?"

Well, yes, the thought had occurred to me on more than one occasion but I wasn't going to admit that to him. Why, I don't know, but I just didn't feel like sharing that priceless bit of information.

He continued, "I'm surprised your rental insurance company hasn't dropped you from your policy."

Sam was starting to annoy me. He was supposed to be here to help or, at least, that's what I had anticipated him doing.

He walked over to the kitchen countertop. "Do I dare ask what this note is about?"

I was so intent on seeing what other damage had been done to my apartment that I hadn't even noticed the note. That's probably the reason why he's a detective and I'm not.

"What does it say?" I asked. Yes, I was nervous. I hoped I wasn't on the Let's-Scare-and-Kill-Harper list.

He glanced over at me and I could tell he was trying hard not to laugh. "Where is it?"

"Where's what, Sam?" I was confused. Well, not so much confused as to wondering what it was he was talking about. Okay, that's what confused means. Words are spinning in my head out of control.

"That's what it says, Harper, 'Where is it?' What do you think that means?"

Oh, I had a pretty good idea. And, it was scary. Did Vykky now think I had the pirate treasure map? How would I have gotten it? The more important thing was: did it really exist?

Something existed, that was for sure, but I didn't know what it was – treasure, Spanish doubloons the pirates had hidden, a map, or something else entirely. Maybe whatever it could be was more valuable than pirate plunder. I couldn't imagine what that might be except maybe valuable real estate.

Contrary to what you might be thinking that's not a far leap...at least not for Florida. Real estate is a very valuable commodity particularly in St. Augustine since there are always ancient artifacts being found. They're also, theoretically, protected by the state but we all know that's not necessarily true.

I personally knew construction people over the years who had found silver and gold coins while they were working on various job sites. Road crew guys found all sorts of things when they were digging in the dirt.

One guy I used to date, before my ex-husband, had found a small chest of silver coins and had sold them to a collector for an obscene amount of money. He basically retired in his thirties until he went fishing on the beautiful St. Johns River, fell in love with the serenity of fishing, and decided to become a fishing tournament professional.

"Harper, did you totally zone out?"

"Huh." That sounded really intelligent but, yes, I had zoned out. I blinked my eyes a couple of times to refocus. "Um, Sam, I have no idea what that note means."

He stared at me for a few minutes and blew his breath out. "Why do I think you're not telling me the truth?"

Grinning inwardly, I have a perverse sense of humor what can I say, and shrugging outwardly. "I don't know what it means."

"Harper, does this have anything to do with Vykky and the Pirate Museum? Cough it up."

"Like a hairball?" I laughed. Apparently, Sam wasn't wearing his sense of humor today.

"Harper," he snapped, "what makes you think Vykky has anything to do with this?"

There was no real concrete evidence that she had anything to do with it except I was sure she was behind it. Then the lightbulb went off in my head.

"Sam," he just looked at me annoyed, "do you remember the last time my apartment was rearranged and you told me to get a surveillance system or at the very least a camera?"

He nodded, still semi-frowning.

"I bought one. It's over there in my African violet pot." I walked over to it and pulled out a teeny tiny little camera. Unless you knew where to look in the plant, no one would ever see it.

A slight smile creased his face but not enough that his dimple showed. "Do I dare ask if we can take a look at it and see who entered your apartment?"

I had two printers next to each other on the little area behind my desk. One was a legitimate printer, the other was my secret hidey-hole spot. I had taken all of the innards out of it and had several things stashed in there including another cell phone. My premise was if something happened to my primary phone

I had a backup with everything already set up in another phone.

On this phone, I could look up the app showing, hopefully, who the intruder was. I punched, I scrolled, and I swiped before the information I wanted showed up.

"Okay, this is interesting," Sam said watching the app's display. "I know who this is."

"Is he a local guy?" I didn't recognize him.

"No." Sam paused, "He's from St. Augustine but he used to come to Palm Park frequently."

"DUI?" I asked. I was starting to guess who it was. The puzzle was starting to come together. I didn't like the picture that was emerging.

Sam ignored me, punched a couple of numbers in his phone, and said, "Raoul Sanchez, b-and-e, Palm Park, he's on camera. He works for Vykky duBorg. Also, suspected for the murder of George Cloises and Todd Stein. Yeah, yeah, okay."

My eyes were the size of saucers. This really was all tied to Vykky. Still, I didn't have a motive or real proof of her involvement. Everything was still very circumstantial.

"Harper, you need to let your attorney know everything."

"Why?" I was truly puzzled. A.B. wasn't going to do anything about this and she wasn't having to bail me out of jail.

Sam didn't answer me. Instead, he took some photos and picked up the note. "Mind if I take this with me?"

"Let me take a picture first." I did.

Sam turned to me as he opened the door, "Call A.B. and tell her what's going on. Tell her I told you to call."

I nodded. Even as squirrelly as my brain cells could be in swirling through the black vortex of life, this really didn't make any sense to me.

Getting the gatekeeper Brenda to let me talk to A.B. proved to be a wee bit of a challenge; however, once I said Sam told me to call her, it was surprising how fast I was able to get through to A.B.

I understand the reason for gatekeepers but it doesn't mean I have to like them.

I thought we had food-bonded over the heavily sugared and calorie-laden doughy delights. Obviously, I was wrong. She couldn't be bribed. No more doughnuts for Brenda.

Relaying everything to A.B., I finally said, "I don't understand why I needed to tell you everything because I don't think any of it really applies to me since I've been cleared on everything thanks to you.

A.B. semi-chuckled. "Life is always interesting, Harper. I'm not sure either unless it's to say Vykky's got something else up her sleeve. Let me know if you hear anything from her."

Chapter 12

My phone went off at two a.m. I wasn't a happy camper. I'm very much a day person. My energy kicks off at five a.m. and doesn't really drain until about eight o'clock at night. Someone calling me at two a.m. had better have a really good reason for calling me at o'dark thirty.

My voice sounded a little raspy as I answered, "Yeah, hello."

"How much?" It was a female's voice but because I was fuzzy from my sleep being interrupted, I wasn't sure who it was calling me. It didn't sound like A.B. or Brenda.

"How much what?" I was trying to sit up in bed and hoping the spun cobwebs in my brain were dissipating. Finally, I was sitting upright with my legs dangling off the edge of the bed. No answer so I repeated my question, "How much what?"

"What do you want? I know you've got it."

Because I had not gotten my eight hours of beauty sleep before being awakened so rudely, I was a wee bit cranky. "Look, whoever you are, you're going to have to be a lot more succinct because I have no clue what you're talking about. If you want me to ghostwrite your book or anything related to writing, talk to my agent. That info is on my website. Good night."

"Stop!" This time the voice was louder and very authoritarian. No doubt about who it was.

"Who do you think you are, Vykky duBorg, calling me at this time of the morning?" I snarled. "I have zero knowledge as to whatever it is and you can call me at a decent hour in the morning. That does not mean seven a.m. either!" I disconnected the call and powered off my phone. I said several not nice things about her ancestry and went back to sleep.

Needing to get back to my book, I was working diligently and realized about noon that I had not had any phone calls or text messages. That was pretty rare because Ronnie and I usually messaged each other a couple times a day. Glancing over at my phone, it suddenly occurred to me that my screen was black; that's when I remembered I had powered down my phone last night. Turning it back on, I saw three calls from an unknown number but no messages and fifty million texts from Ronnie. The last one said, "gurl where u b i worried bringing pizza at 1230 2 make sure u ok."

I heard borderline frantic knocking at my door. I scurried across the living room and opened the door.

Ronnie threw his arms around me while holding a hot pizza box in one hand. "Oh, honey, honey! I'm so glad you're okay! I was worried sick about you!"

He was such a good guy and I knew how fortunate I was to have a great friend like him. I smiled, "Let me tell you about last night."

Placing the pizza box on the countertop and flipping open the lid, he said, "Did you have a special night with a hottie detective?"

I couldn't help it, I started to laugh. "Oh, I wish! But, no." And then I proceeded to tell him about Vykky calling me, all of the calls this morning, and finished with, "She must be desperate, otherwise, she wouldn't be calling me like this."

Scarfing down another slice of pepperoni pizza, he said, "Sure sounds like it, doesn't it? Harper, should you call A.B. and tell her what's going on? Isn't this harassment?"

I shook my head. "Probably not because she's not leaving any messages and it's circumstantial as to who it is making the calls."

Picking up a slice, I glanced over at him. "No PMS special – pepperoni, mushrooms, and sausage?"

"Honey, I was just so nervous about you that I don't think I could have eaten anything other than pepperoni." He was reaching for a third piece. I shudder to think how many slices he could have eaten if he weren't nervous. I've seen the man consume an entire large pizza by himself...and not gain an ounce.

My phone rang with Unknown Caller on the I.D. Pointing at the screen, "Gotta be Vykky."

Wiping my hands on a paper towel, I didn't want to get pizza grease on my phone, I answered on the third ring. "Hello."

"Where is it?" The voice was flat, slightly irritated, and demanding.

"Vykky, I have absolutely no clue what you're talking about." I had put her on speaker and motioned to Ronnie to be quiet. "Would you care to enlighten me as to what you think I have or know about?"

I could hear her tapping her nails. She must have me on speaker phone as well. She might have been debating what to share.

"I want the map and I want the silver bars."

Ronnie and I looked at each other, our eyes wide. So there was a treasure map and pirate plunder.

"Vykky, what on God's green earth makes you think I have any of that? More importantly, how would I have gotten that from George?" I was trying to sound a little peeved but it came out more like I was seriously annoyed, borderline angry.

She ignored my questions. "How much do you want? Name a price."

Ronnie poked me, his eyes still the size of dinner plates, and he was rubbing his fingers together indicating big money.

"You're a businessperson, Vykky, so what's the real reason why you want the map and the treasure? Is it for the notoriety? Are you going to sell bits and pieces of it for outrageous prices? Is it for your own private collection or..." a thought just occurred to me and I snapped my fingers, "are you the middleman and selling it to someone else?"

While I personally didn't know anyone with millions and millions of dollars who could buy the Spanish artifacts, I did strongly suspect Vykky did.

There was a long pause then, "What I want it for is none of your business. How much?"

I had to give the woman credit where credit was due, she was focused on what she wanted.

"Why did you send Raoul to trash my apartment?" Enquiring minds wanted to know.

"Who?"

Now I was angry. I don't get angry very often simply because I'm lazy and don't want to waste my energy on negative things. "Stop pretending you don't know who he is, Vykky. In fact, since you are apparently exhibiting signs of dementia, let me refresh your memory."

I took a deep breath, "Raoul is your landscaping all-around handyman who you bought a house for his mother after you helped get them out of Venezuela. He's been with you for years.

"More importantly, I have him on camera breaking and entering my apartment and trashing my place."

"What someone in my employ does on their off time is none of my business." She was haughty to the core. Sad to say, she was going to throw a loyal employee under the bus and let law enforcement do what they wanted with him. Providing for his mom to continue to live in the lifestyle she had become accustomed was probably a very small price to pay for Raoul's silence. I wasn't a fan of that school of thought; however, I wasn't as successful a businessperson as Vykky and she probably simply considered this as a cost of doing business. I still wasn't a fan of doing this to someone regardless of how pretty the package was with a big red bow tied around it.

She wasn't going to admit to anything.

"So, how much?"

I sighed, "Vykky, I truly do not know anything about a map or treasure. I was really just doing research at the Pirate Museum. I don't know what George knew or found. I'm truly not interested in the pirate treasure, although if you wanted to throw some bucks my way, that would be great."

The phone disconnected.

Chapter 13

Vykky was irritated and tapping her red lacquered nails on her desk. Her personal phone rang.

"So did you decide on a price?" she asked.

"This isn't Harper, Vykky."

"Why are you bothering me now? The game's not over yet."

"Vykky, Vykky, Vykky…"

"I hate it when you do that." She was livid.

"You weren't supposed to murder anyone, much less two people. George really would have told you I have the map and the treasure which, by the way, is on property I own."

"How long have you had the map?" It suddenly occurred to Vykky that she had been played.

"Oh, for quite a while now but, Vykky, the map's not what is the most important thing." The caller paused, "The most important thing is the treasure chest that was filled with gold, silver, gems, and jewelry. Vykky, it was all the way to the top. It was packed."

"How much?" Vykky's voice was frosty.

"It's not for sale and, even if it were, you don't have that type of money. The land's not for sale either." Another pause, "You cheated, Vykky. You weren't supposed to kill anyone."

She huffed, "I'll have you know I didn't kill anyone."

"You're talking semantics, Vykky. You didn't kill someone directly, but you ordered it. Same thing."

"How did you get the map and find the treasure?"

"My secret." There was a soft giggle.

"Wait! How long have you had the map?"

"Well, cuz, for quite a long while." There was a pause, then a smirk. "Let me think for a moment. Oh, yes, I've had it for a couple of years. When you attended Flagler College and you had that little incident with the board of directors, your mother apparently decided you couldn't be trusted, and she gave the map to my mother."

Vykky gasped. "My, my mother had the map?"

"Um, humm, she gave it to my mother and..."

"My mother hated your mother!" Vykky almost screamed into the phone.

"True but they had made an agreement, a legal agreement, that whichever one of their daughters could figure out where Kidd's treasure was buried, they could have it."

Vykky was breathing heavily into the phone, not saying anything.

"Vykky, you knew the rules of the game. Find the map, find the treasure, no killing. You didn't do either of the first two things and you did have two men killed. You lose. I have the map and I have the treasure."

Hissing, Vykky said, "I've looked for that map for years. You won't get away with this! Kidd's treasure is mine."

"You underestimated me, cuz." The voice was taunting now. "It was so easy to have George tease you with a map that didn't exist and to give you a couple of doubloons."

"You played me, Anne Bonny Mary Read!" screamed Vykky.

"It's all about the game, Vykky. You know that. Please, call me A.B. everyone else does."

Vykky was seething. "I'll kill you personally! I'm not hiring anyone to do my dirty work this time."

"Vykky," A.B.'s voice was soft, "didn't your mother ever tell you to not mess with a woman with two female pirate names? Goodbye."

Turning to Detective Sam Needles, A.B. said, "I think you've got enough to arrest her now."

He nodded. Looking around A.B.'s law office with all of the pirate portraits, maps, and artifacts, he said, "Love how you've decorated the place, A.B. Any of it real?"

A.B. grinned, "What do you think?"

Chapter 14

I had taken coffee over to Ronnie at the pet store. I needed a Maltese puppy fix with their cute little faces and personalities, not to mention their soft fur and little kisses.

"Can you believe it, honey? I had no clue A.B. and Vykky were related." Ronnie was holding up a newspaper where the headlines proclaimed Vykky's arrest in big letters. That was not a flattering picture of her on the front page.

I agreed. "I didn't either. This only goes to show you what greed can do to a person. A.B. comes out looking like a champ."

Ronnie grinned, "So does your hottie, Detective Sam."

Blushing, I said, "Well, we kinda do have a dinner date tonight."

High fiving me, he only said, "Life is always good in Palm Park."

Looking for a dash of fun, a hint of snark, a sprinkle of sass, and a whole lot of silliness with a Florida twist?

SCAN ME!

To receive a FREE Book

Join my free, no obligation, twice a month newsletter, and I promise not to send your email address to the "your car warranty has expired" people

SharonEBuck.com

Purchase my books at your favorite retailer

SHARON E. BUCK
A Harper Rogers Cozy Mystery
MURDER AT PALM PARK

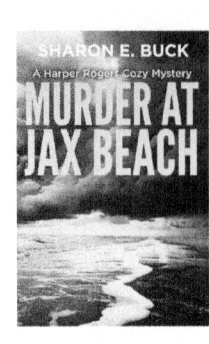

SHARON E. BUCK
A Harper Rogers Cozy Mystery
MURDER AT JAX BEACH

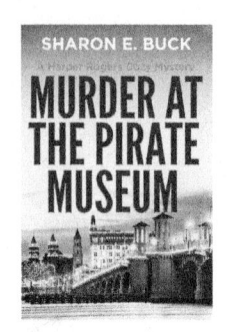

SHARON E. BUCK
A Harper Rogers Cozy Mystery
MURDER AT THE PIRATE MUSEUM

For the Parker Bell & Lady Gatorettes series, turn the page.

Purchase my books at your favorite retailer

Book 1
A Dose of Nice and Murder

Book 2
A Honky Tonk Night and Murder

Book 3
The Faberge Easter Egg and Murder

Book 4
Little Candy Hearts and Murder

Book 5
Lights, Action, Camera and Murder

Book 6
A Turkey Parade and Murder

Book 7
Cookies and Murder

Book 8
Flamingos and Murder

Book 9
Bowling and Murder

Purchase my books at your favorite retailer

101 Summer Jobs for Teachers

Kids Fun Activity Book

Counting Laughs

Acknowledgements

Thank you to my wonderful support team and friends for your encouragement, words of reassurance, inspiration, and belief in me on those days when the blank computer screen would stare back at me like a one-eyed monster daring me not to write anything. I survived and conquered.

In no special order, thanks to the following individuals:

Cindy Stavely at The Pirate Museum in St. Augustine for her kindness in letting me view and take notes of The Pirate Museum. This is a fun adventure for your family, friends, or even just by yourself. Visit ThePirateMuseum.com

Kim Steadman – There should be a law about how much we're allowed to laugh on the phone. You get me. Thank you for your friendship, and the time we spend talking about writing, ideas, books, ideas, the book business, ideas, laughing, ideas, and just chatting. Did I mention ideas? "Focus, Sharon, focus" and "Keep the main thing, the main thing." Visit KimSteadman.com

Bellamina Court – Who would have ever thunk that we would hit it off as author sisters Inkers Con 2024? We may have been twins at birth who were inadvertently separated at birth by different mothers hundreds of miles away.

We are like two peas in a pod in so many ways. Thanks for all the laughs, giggles, and just sheer silliness we come up with in addition to all of our writing escapades. You get it. Thanks for the unique spelling of Vykky for this book and the great tagline for About the Author. Visit BellaminaCourt.com

Terezia Barna – Thank you for your encouragement, kindness, laughter, and phenomenal email program. Visit TereziaBarna.com

Cindy Marvin – My friend and attorney who tries (hard) to keep me out of trouble before I even get into it. She may or may not be a character in this book. Interestingly enough, her dad went by A.B. And, no, I did not know that when

I wrote the book.

Michelle Margiotta – Your music has lifted me up when I was frustrated with my writing process, when I had doubts, and it has nurtured the very depths of my soul. Your music is so filled with colors and swirls dancing throughout your compositions that one cannot help but be totally enthralled and inspired by your incredible gift. Visit MichelleMargiotta.com

George and Mama at Athenian Owl Restaurant – Yes, there really is a George and Mama! And, yes, George really is a Greek Adonis. My favorite Greek restaurant in Jacksonville and they make me feel at home every time I eat there. Visit Athenian Owl

And, lastly, thank you to all my loyal readers and fans. I love and appreciate you!

To God be the glory.

About the author

Hi, Friend,

Yes, we're now friends because you were kind enough to buy this book and I want you to know how much I appreciate that!

You know how most authors write dull, boring, "this is about me" author bios? Yeah, well, that's not me. I do a lot of fun, silly, off-the-wall crazy stuff, and funny seems to follow me everywhere. I'm happy to share funny with you and, hopefully, make you grin or laugh...thus, interrupting the craziness of your everyday life. Blatant plug, hop on over to my website and sign up for my twice-a-month newsletter (you'll also receive a free book) SharonEBuck.com

Sleuthing off for now with a wink and a clue. May the snark be with you.

Sharon

Printed in Dunstable, United Kingdom